Leon's Song

For Jeff, Sarah, Eryn and Tristan
Stephanie

To my husband Lee and my new baby girl, Ekko Lee
Dianna

Text copyright © 2004 by Stephanie McLellan
Illustrations copyright © 2004 by Dianna Bonder

Published in Canada by Fitzhenry & Whiteside,
195 Allstate Parkway, Markham, Ontario L3R 4T8

Published in the United States by Fitzhenry & Whiteside,
121 Harvard Avenue, Suite 2, Allston, Massachusetts 02134

www.fitzhenry.ca   godwit@fitzhenry.ca

10 9 8 7 6 5 4 3 2 1

National Library of Canada Cataloguing in Publication

McLellan, Stephanie Simpson,
Leon's song / Stephanie McLellan ; [illustrated by] Dianna Bonder.

ISBN 1-55041-813-0

I. Bonder, Dianna, 1970- II. Title.

PS8575.L457L45 2004   jC813'.6   C2004-901914-7

U.S. Publisher Cataloging-in-Publication Data
(Library of Congress Standards)

McLellan, Stephanie.
Leon's song / Stephanie McLellan ; Dianna Bonder. –1st ed.
[32] p. : col. ill. ; cm.
Summary: Humble Leon is an old frog who accepts his shortcomings.
He longs only to sing beautifully. But when his friends are in danger,
the old frog's bravery reveals a great talent that brings him more fame
than he's ever dreamt about.
ISBN 1-55041-813-0
1. Frogs — Fiction — Juvenile literature. 2. Friends — Fiction – Juvenile literature.
3. Bravery — Fiction — Juvenile literature. I. Bonder, Dianna. I. Title.
[E] dc22   PZ7.M354Le 2004

Fitzhenry & Whiteside acknowledges with thanks the Canada Council for the Arts,
the Government of Canada through the Book Publishing Industry Development Program (BPIDP),
and the Ontario Arts Council for their support of our publishing program.

Design by Wycliffe Smith
Printed in Hong Kong

Leon's Song

by Stephanie Simpson McLellan

Illustrated by Dianna Bonder

Fitzhenry & Whiteside

Leon was an old frog. Forty times he'd seen his pond freeze in winter and forty springs had thawed his world awake. Forty years is a long time for a frog.

If you saw Leon dozing in the sun, you might think age had made him all quiet and peaceful inside. You might think he was content to spend his days resting and remembering. But you'd be wrong.

As old as Leon was, his heart was young with yearning. All his life, Leon had longed to do something important—something that would make a difference in the world.

The trouble was, Leon didn't have any special talents. To make things worse, he was a bit of a coward. He avoided dark shadows and jumped at sudden noises. He always had the uncomfortable feeling that something strange and terrible was about to happen. All this fretting made Leon watchful and careful, but it didn't make him special.

Despite his fears, Leon felt sure that he had been born for a purpose, and the older he got, the more he thought about it.

Early one hot August morning, Leon sat in a shady hollow watching the pond wake up. He smiled at the sight of Orlando striking a pose atop his lily pad while admiring his reflection. Orlando was a handsome frog. He was sleek and smooth, and rather imposing. Leon stared at his own reflection, which was lumpy and bumpy and kind of fat. He smiled again. Beauty wasn't Leon's gift. And he was all right with that.

Leon plopped into the pond for an early morning swim. Suddenly he was sent spinning as a lithe frog hurtled past him. Marco was the fastest swimmer in the pond. Kicking out his creaky frog's legs, Leon thought about shooting through the water after Marco. But swimming fast wasn't Leon's gift. And he was all right with that.

Breaking the surface, Leon saw young Alonzo leap clear from one shore to the other. Leon felt an itch in his feet and a twitch in his legs, and for a second, he almost tried the same phenomenal jump. Leon chuckled to himself. Wouldn't that be something for such an old frog! Even in his prime he'd never jumped as far as Alonzo could.

Jumping wasn't Leon's gift. And he was all right with that.

But when Leon caught sight of Romeo swimming out from the cattails toward the center of the pond, a sharp ache replaced the old frog's smile. Romeo was a singer, and there was no other his equal.

As Romeo breathed a slow, sad song to the still, hot air, the little fishes raised their heads above the pond's surface and swayed to the gentle beat.

The dragonflies hummed
in slow rhythms around the
lily pads and even the tiny
tadpoles swam lazily on the
pond's surface, making idle ripples
that caressed the water beetles
and the swimming spiders.

As Romeo's tempo quickened, his high, happy notes enticed a light breeze out of the still, thick air, and the little fishes leapt out of the water with joyful exuberance. The sun caught the spray of water, which flew in circles around their glistening fish bodies and made a hundred little rainbows. The dragonflies swerved and dipped in intricate, shimmery patterns in the hot summer air. Even the tiny tadpoles blipped crazily along the surface like a million joyous raindrops.

Like the others, Leon was profoundly moved by Romeo's singing, which seemed so much more important than beauty or power or physical strength. With all his heart Leon wished he had such a voice. There was nothing he longed for more.

Yet as sad and small as his lack of talent made him feel, Leon was deeply inspired by Romeo's low, throaty rumblings and high, thin trills. While the other pond creatures swayed and shimmered and danced, Leon closed his eyes, his heart swelling with possibility.

But something else was raised by Romeo's beautiful strains.
Something large and unfamiliar. A dark shadow advanced beneath
the surface, deliberate and undetected.

Leon alone was gripped by the feeling that something was about
to change the world. He opened his eyes and, seeing the approaching
shadow, became cold with fear.

At first Leon didn't know what he was looking at, but then
he saw the menacing fin, the ragged whiskers, the jagged teeth.
As the creature continued to glide silently toward his friends,
Leon didn't stop to wonder how such a monstrous fish had
come to be in their pond.

Out of nowhere, Leon found his voice. Though cracked and dry and uneven, his song was loud and passionate, filled with a commanding urgency.

It was the biggest sound the pond had ever heard.

He sang until his friends stopped and listened and understood.

The little fishes darted quickly, deep and far away. The dragonflies zoomed up into the trees. Even the tiny tadpoles wiggled away to safety.

Without thinking, Leon leaped right on top of the big, ugly fish. From their hiding places, all the pond dwellers were astonished at how imposing Leon looked as he filled himself with air atop this monster a hundred times his size.

Leon bellowed out another loud, menacing note, and the big fish bolted away in fear. Swimming after the creature, Leon continued to sing. Powerful sound waves rumbled through the water, touching every heart and every shore. As the fish darted into an underwater cavern, the power of Leon's song tumbled heavy boulders over the entrance, sealing it off forever.

When Leon returned, everyone was waiting for him. The little fishes swam admiringly in circles around him. The dragonflies made the air vibrate with excitement, and the tiny tadpoles caressed his lumpy, bumpy body with adoration. They all begged Leon to sing to them, and when his dry, cracked voice echoed shyly across the still water, every heart was moved by the hidden beauty it contained.

As everyone replayed the events in their minds, a reverent hush settled over the pond. Never had Alonzo seen such a powerful leap, or Marco such a forceful swim. Orlando gazed at Leon, struck by how imposing he had looked.

Romeo bowed deeply to the old frog, and the others followed. The passionate strains of Leon's song would echo forever in Romeo's ears.

Leon lived for many happy years after that. Yet even after he was gone, generations told the story of what might have been lost but wasn't. They sang Leon's song, remembering what a difference it had made to them all.